# Paddington

at the Fair

# Michael Bond

# Paddington

## at the Fair

## illustrated by R.W. ALLEY

HarperCollins *Children's Books*

One day in summer the Browns went on an outing to a part of London called Hampstead, where there was a big fair.

Paddington had never been to a fair before and he was most excited.

Mr Brown gave Jonathan, Judy and
Paddington a pound each. "I should make
the most of it," he said. "The fair only
happens once a year."

First of all, Paddington had
a go on the Coconut Shy.
He hit the man in
charge by mistake.

"That isn't a very good start," said Mrs
Brown.

"Perhaps you should stand on something,"
suggested Judy.

Paddington thought that was a very good idea, and stood on his brown suitcase. After two more goes he had won a china bird for his bedroom wall and a picture of a goldfish.

"I shall call the goldfish Hampstead," he said, "after the fair."

And he gave his prizes to Mrs Bird to
hold so that he could have a ride on
the carousel.

Paddington enjoyed the carousel so
much he went on it a second time.

"I think it's a very good way of
travelling if you don't want to go
anywhere," he called as he went past.
"Especially if you have plenty
of marmalade
sandwiches to
keep you going."
While he was on the carousel, Paddington
noticed the Helter-skelter and he was soon
on his way up with a mat.

"Did you enjoy that?" asked Mr Brown.

"Yes, thank you very much," said Paddington. "But it was a very quick way of spending fifty pence."

"That's funny," said Mrs Brown, looking up. "None of the other children are coming down. They all seem to be stuck."

"Oh, dear," said Paddington. "I think they may be sitting on one of my marmalade sandwiches."

"Perhaps we'd better go on the Space Craft before they find out," said Jonathan hastily.

Paddington liked anything new and he quickly climbed into an empty car.

He soon wished he hadn't. One moment they were climbing slowly up towards the sky. The next moment they came shooting back down again at breakneck speed.

SPACE
CRAFT

The cars went up and down and round and round. There were times when it felt as if they were going upside down as well.

"I wish I had chosen a different car," he groaned as they climbed out. "Mine felt as if it was trying to throw me out."

"I think they all felt the same," said Judy.

"Perhaps you should ask for your money back," joked Mr Brown, as he helped Paddington to his feet.

"I may ask for my stomach back," said Paddington darkly.

"How about trying something a bit quieter for a change?" said Mrs Brown.

"I don't think you'll find those very quiet!" called Jonathan.

But he was too late. Paddington was already climbing into a Dodgem car.

He soon found out why some people call them 'Bumper cars'.

By the time Paddington came off the Dodgem cars it was getting late and he had spent nearly all his money.

Just then he saw a tent with a notice outside which said:

Madame GRANT

FORTUNES TOLD

"Perhaps she will tell me where my next pound coin is coming from," he said, and before the Browns could stop him he had gone inside.

Madame Grant looked at Paddington, then
she looked into her crystal ball. Then she
looked at Paddington again.

It was very hot inside the tent and
Paddington had his eyes closed.

"I think," she said, "I see a bear who
is going to sleep very well tonight."

And she was quite right. Paddington slept very well that night. In fact he slept so well he didn't fall out of bed once; not even when he dreamed he was back on the Space Craft.

Hampstead Fish

First published in hardback in Great Britain by HarperCollins*Publishers* in 1985
First published in paperback by Collins Picture Books in 2000
Published as part of a gift set by HarperCollins Children's Books in 2007

5 7 9 10 8 6 4

Collins Picture Books is an imprint of the Children's Division, part of HarperCollins Publishers Ltd.
HarperCollins Children's Books is a division of HarperCollins Publishers Ltd.

Text copyright © Michael Bond 1985
Illustrations copyright © R.W. Alley 1998

Visit our website at: www.harpercollins.co.uk

Printed and bound in China